STAYING
alive

JAMES GOODENOUGH

ISBN 978-1-63525-776-2 (Paperback)
ISBN 978-1-63525-777-9 (Digital)

Christian Faith Publishing, Inc.
296 Chestnut Street
Meadville, PA 16335
www.christianfaithpublishing.com

Printed in the United States of America

In loving memory of my daughter
MyRanda
May she rest in peace.

One hot day in April, I came home early to surprise my wife, Rona. She was a retired supermodel, and I was a disabled cop from an injury five years ago that put me out of work. I wanted to have some alone time with her. Our kids were out with their friends and wouldn't be back till late evening. My wife told me my old friend Dan, whom I've known for about fifteen years, had called and wanted me to call him as soon as I got in.

Jimmy: I'll call later. I want to go to our room and cuddle and make love to you.

Later that afternoon, I called Dan.

Jimmy: Hey, what's up, Dan? I heard you called me today.
Dan: Yeah, remember that car you bought a few months back that you told me about?
Jimmy: Yes.
Dan: Well, when I came into work today, I got a report in on a green '72 Impala, that the car was stolen in Louisiana, and I know that you bought a green '72, so I called to see if it was the same one. By the way, do you know where the car came from?
Jimmy: No, but I have the VIN in my safe, I can go get it. Here, ************. Go see if it's the same on the report, and call me later and let me know.

Dan: Hold on, I got the report here, and yes, it's a match. OK, we have two choices: one, we come and pick it up and do a whole lot of paper work, or two, you can call David at ***-***-**** and see if you can work it out.

Jimmy: Then I will call him and see what he says.

Dan: Hey, Jimmy, call me and let me know what you worked out, and I'll try to help if I can.

Jimmy: OK, I will, and thanks for the heads up, my friend.

Dan: No problem, I know you'd do it for me, 'bye.

Jimmy: 'Bye.

Rona came into my den and asked me: So what was so important for you to call him?

Jimmy: You're not going to believe this, that car I sank a lot of money on for repairs and got it running, it was stolen a few months ago!

Rona: But don't you have the title?

Jimmy: Yes, but if the car is stolen and then sold, it still belongs to the owner, so I'll call David and see if we can buy it from him.

Later that night, I called David.

Jimmy: Hello?

David: Hello.

Jimmy: This is Jimmy, a friend at the police department called me and told me about your car that I bought a few months ago and that you reported it stolen.

David: Yes, I did. I just got out of the hospital and my car was gone, and I called the police.

Jimmy: Well, sir, will you consider selling me the car? I've done a lot of work to repair it, 'cause when I got, the car it was damaged.

David: No, it's my only car. I'm an old man and that's how I get around town.

Jimmy: I'll pay you a fair price.

Rona, came into my den and heard me tell David about buying it: What about all the money we put into it? Ask him that. (I wave her away.)

David: I don't care. That car was my deceased wife's car, I want it back.

Jimmy: I understand, but my wife is right, I think we could work out an arrangement that we both can live with.

David: Or I can give the cops up here your number, and see how that works out for ya.

Jimmy: Yes, you can, but I would like to see if we can both benefit out of this.

David: Look, I'm on a fix income and don't have a lot of money to give.

Jimmy: OK, I understand and that's why i said i buy it from you.

David: I said no are you going to bring me my car or not.

Jimmy: OK, I don't want to make you upset, I do want this car but if you say no, then I will have to live with that answer, and I tell you what I do for you, a good deed, and I'll bring it to you so we don't have to get the police involved any more than we have to, OK?

David: OK, as long as you get my car back to me in a week, then I'll call the police and drop the stolen-car charges, OK?

Jimmy: OK, where do you live at? I'll leave in the morning.

David: I live at 555 Palm Street in Jefferson County, a small town in Louisiana, just outside of New Orleans.

Jimmy: OK, I'll see you soon. 'Bye for now.

David: 'Bye.

Jimmy went to where Rona is and tells her that they have to make a road trip.

Rona: We can't, the kids still have school. It's the end of the year, and they can't miss any school.

Jimmy: We don't have a choice, we don't have the money for a plane or a bus for me to get back here on, so the kids would have to come with us. This way we have the van to come home in, and

besides, with you in the van, there'd be no one to take care of
the kids.

Rona: What about Dan? He's your friend, right?

Jimmy: Yes, but he is single, and the kids don't need to be around
his bar-hopping and one-night-stands. If he gets a case for a
stakeout then he'd be on the spot and will have to do something
with our kids.

Rona: OK, then I guess they're coming with us.

Jimmy: And besides, we can stop by your mom's place and the kids
can see Grandma.

Rona: They'd like that, it's been such a long time since the last time
we've gone up there. So how long do we have?

Jimmy: David said he'd give me a week to get the car up to him. In
the morning, we can pack the van and call Dan and let him
know what we are doing, and then go to the bank and get some
money for the trip.

Rona: Well, we better get to bed so we can get well rested for tomorrow because I know how you are—the crack of dawn, you'd be
up and making noise, honey.

Jimmy: Yes, dear, you are right, I do get up early.

Rona: So I'll call the parents that the kids are staying at and get the
kids to come home and let the kids know about the road trip.

About an hour went by when the Bowkers showed up with our
kids. MyRanda, who had just turned eighteen; Amanda, thirteen;
Deanna, nine; and our son, Mike, six, had been all invited for a
hangout with their friends Scott, Jenna, and Adam. They had a pool
and were going to have pizza delivered and had planned to hang out
till evening.

Rona: Did you all have a good time at your friend's house?

Amanda: Yeah, Mom, it was great! They had pizza, and we played
in the pool, and Scott kept doing belly flops and getting our
hair wet, and Jenna was yelling at him, but Scott kept it up till
his dad came out and told him to play nice or he'd have to go
inside. Adam played with Mike in the sandbox, and they made

a race track for their Hot Wheels. Their mom was on the lawn chair to keep an eye on us, but we had fun.

MyRanda: So why did we have to come home early?

Rona: MyRanda, we will talk about it in a few, OK? You all get ready for bed, and we will come in and talk and tuck you in, OK?

MyRanda: Me too?

Rona: Yes, MyRanda, you too.

Jimmy: Sorry you had to bring them home so soon. We have to go out of town, and we need to get to bed so we can get an early start in the morning.

Ken: Oh, OK. Did something happen?

Jimmy: Yeah. (We tell them the whole story.)

Elaine: Oh my god. Well, be safe and let us know if you need anything. If we can, we'll try to help.

Rona: OK, but the kids will get to see their grandma, so it's not a total loss.

Elaine: Let your kids know that they are going on a road trip to see Grandma.

Rona: OK, we will, and we'll see you in a week.

Ken: OK, 'bye, call you later, OK?

Rona and Jimmy: OK, 'bye.

Rona: Honey, you lock up, and I'll be in the girl's room.

Jimmy: OK, I'll be in there in a minute.

Rona went to MyRanda's room and was talking to her when Dad walked in, and he explained what's going on.

MyRanda: Why can't I stay home? I'm old enough.

Rona: Yes, you are, but I thought you might want to see Grandma.

MyRanda: Yes, it's been a minute since I've seen her.

Rona: OK then, when you get up, can you help us get things packed and your sisters ready for the trip?

MyRanda: Of course, Mom, I'll help.

Rona: Amanda, would you like to see Grandma too?

Amanda: Yeah, no school and we're going to Grandma's!

Rona: Well, that sounds like a yes to me. Here, lie down (kisses Amanda on the head). Now, we have a big day tomorrow, get some sleep.

Deanna and you: *Zzz, zzz, zzz.*

Jimmy: She already asleep, let's go and put Mike in bed.

Rona: OK.

Jimmy: Boy, it's time to get in bed. Do you remember Grandma?

Mike: I think so.

Rona: Well, we are going to see her tomorrow, and we have to go somewhere else, so can you get in bed and go to sleep because tomorrow we're getting up early, and it's going to be a long day. We need to pack, can you help out in the morning?

Mike: OK, Mom and Dad, I will (kiss on the head).

Rona: OK, let me tuck you in. Goodnight, get to sleep.

Beep-beep-beep-beep, it's 5:00 AM.

Jimmy: Yeah, I'm up (*click*). OK, better get the coffee ready and see what we have to do to get ready to get on the road. OK, let's see, I'll make breakfast and then get everyone up.

As the house fills up with the coffee and bacon smell, everyone starts to come out of their rooms.

Deanna: It smells good, Dad, when will it be done?

Jimmy: In five minutes. Deanna. Go see if your mom's up yet, and let her know breakfast is about done.

Deanna: OK. Mom, Mommy, are you up? It's time to eat, come on, I'm hungry!

Rona: Yeah, I'm up, getting dressed. I'll be in there in a minute, OK?

Deanna: I'll tell Dad. Daddy, Mom's on her way.

Jimmy: OK. MyRanda, get the table set and get the kids at the table.

MyRanda: OK, Dad, I will.

As we all sat at the table and thanked the Lord for the food, we explained what's going on and that's why we all were going on the road trip.

Jimmy: OK, kids, let's get the car packed, and make sure we turn everything off and close and lock all the doors. I'll go and talk to the neighbor and let him know we'll be gone for a week or so.

Rona: Well, what did Gerry say?

Jimmy: He will watch our place and call the police if he sees anything. OK, kids, we need to get in the van, get going, and if anyone wants to ride with me, speak up now.

Rona: Honey, you take your son and have someone on one time with him.

Jimmy: OK, Mike, looks like you get to hang with Dad. We're going to the bank and then hit the highway.

While we were at the bank, Rona asked if I had called Dan and let him know we were leaving.

Jimmy: Yeah, I called him at his house a few minutes ago.

It's been two hours now, and we made it to Texas. In four hours, we would be at Grandma's place, and with all the stops, it would be four o'clock before we get there.

Jimmy: Of course she's not home. Hey, Rona, did you call your mom?

Rona: No, I wanted to surprise her.

Jimmy: Well, I guess we got the surprise, huh!

Rona: Jimmy, stop.

Jimmy: What? All I'm saying is, she's not here. Let's go and get something to eat and come back later, OK?

Rona: Yeah, the kids need to get out and stretch their legs anyway, so where are we going to go and get some food?

Jimmy: Dairy Queen, and then we can go to a park and eat and walk around for a few.

About 7:00 PM, we went back to Grandma's house. As I pulled up, I blew the horn; I knew that she hated that. As Patty came out, the kids ran up to her.

Kids: Grandma, we've came to see you.

Patty: Ya'll come on inside, and we can talk in there. Grandpa is inside cleaning his guns, be careful.

Patty leans over to Rona and asks: So what's with the visit? Not that I mind you coming, it's just out of the blue.

Rona: If we stay the night, we'll let you know after the kids go to sleep.

Patty: OK, ya'll hungry?

Kids: Naw, we ate at the park. Do you have ice cream, Grandma?

Patty: No, but I have watermelon, you want that? But you have to eat it outside.

Kids: OK, yeah, yeah! Yes, please.

Patty: Boy, you are so sweet.

Jimmy, walking in and seeing Roger sitting there, cleaning his shotgun and a few other guns: Hey, Dad, came down for a flyby and brought the kids to see ya'll.

Roger: Hey, you want a beer? You're not driving anymore tonight, right?

Jimmy: No, we are staying the night.

Roger: Come on, let's go out back and toss a few back.

Jimmy: Sure. Hon, me and Dad going out back, OK.

Now me and Roger have always gotten along, but for some reason, my mother-in-law has hated my guts from day one (not sure why), but we don't talk, or if we do, we bicker at each other as I was out back. I told Roger what's going on and that we hope that it all goes smooth.

Roger: You want to take one of my guns?

Jimmy: Naw, I got my old service gun in the van if we need it.

Roger: OK, I got this new .40 caliber that's awesome, with a seventeen-shot clip.

Jimmy: Thanks, Dad, but no, we shouldn't need it.

Roger: OK, let's get inside and let Mom know what's going on.

Rona came outside as we were walking up the stairs.

Rona: You guys coming in or what?

Jimmy: Yeah, we were about to walk in now.

Rona: Grandma told the kids that it's late and they all need to go to bed, and two of the kids can sleep in the guest living room.

Jimmy and Roger got back in the house and sat down, and started to tell her mom what was happening.

Patty: Hold it, let me guess, your dipshit of a husband done f—— shit up again, and now ya'll in deep shit.

Jimmy: Hey, I'm not to blame for this, you old hag. This is totally out of my control, shit happens.

Rona: Mom, can you be nice to my husband? And you stop calling her hag.

In the meantime, Roger is sitting over in the corner, laughing his ass off.

Patty: Listen here, you little shit, I'll blow your nuts off if you call me that again (pulls out a .9 mm). Push it, sonny, and you better stop blowing your horn every time you come here!

Jimmy: See, dear, I didn't start it, and she keeps pushing my buttons every time. I don't know why, but I keep thinking she's changed every time I come here.

Rona: I know, honey, she's just set in her ways and you just got to let it go.

Jimmy: Better yet, why doesn't she just tell me what the hell the problem is that she has with me and then we can go from there?

Patty: You really want to know? Really? OK. About nineteen years ago, my baby was modeling, and you came along, a snot-nose rookie cop, and got my baby to stop her modeling by getting her pregnant. And we all know once a model has a baby, their career is through, and sure as shit, that's what happened. Listen, we love our grandbabies, but I think it could have waited a few years. You were in your prime, and now look at you, you can't go back.

Rona: Ma, you can't hold that against him. We were in love, and love has no boundaries. You need to let it go.

Patty. Not till the day I die.

Jimmy: There you have it, we just won't talk then.

Patty: It sounds good to me.

Roger: Well, son, I'll still talk to you.

Jimmy: Thanks, Dad, I appreciate that.

Rona continued with her tale, and Mom surprised me for the first time ever.

Patty: The kids can stay here till you get done, and on your way back, pick them back up.

Dad stands up and says: Well, what time are you leaving in the morning?

Rona: About six, right, honey?

Jimmy: Yes, dear, I was thinking that's a good time to beat the traffic.

Patty: OK, let's all get to bed, and Jimmy, you can sleep outside.

Rona: Mom, stop, he'll sleep with me, or are you going make me sleep outside!

Patty: No, and no sex in the house. I don't want to hear that noise.

Rona: Honey, shut up, don't even say a thing.

Jimmy: What? All I was going to say was, "Yes, ma'am."

Rona: You were not, don't lie. OK, we'll sleep in the other room.

The next morning I, got up and went and got everyone else up except Mom and Dad. I told everyone: Be quiet till later, Grandma and Pa are still asleep. I'll make breakfast, and they'll wake up to the smell in the house.

About twenty minutes later, Grandma came out, and right off the bat—

Patty: Who in the hell told you can cook in my house? Get the f——— out of my kitchen!

Jimmy: Instead, why don't you sit down and let me finish cooking, hag.

Patty: Look, you stupid shit, my house, my rules. Now get the f—— out of the way.

Amanda: Why are you yelling at Dad? Did he do something wrong?

Patty: No, it's just I don't like waking up and seeing someone in my kitchen.

Deanna: We are sorry, we were hungry and didn't think you'd get mad at us.

Patty: I'm not mad, it's just I cook in my own house. Ya'll go sit down.

Rona: See, Mom, this is what I've been telling you about on the phone, you need to stop in front of the kids.

Patty looks at me and said: You're right, I will try.

Rona: That's all I'm asking.

Patty: You get this one (gives Jimmy a titty-twister).

Jimmy: Ouch, that hurts!

Rona: Mom, stop, and you, Jimmy, go back to the stove.

Grandpa comes out and says: What's all the noise about?

Amanda: Grandma is mad at Dad 'cause he's cooking.

Roger: No, I don't think that's it. She's just grumpy when she gets up, OK?

Grandma: Why don't you find something on the TV for the kids, and I'll go talk to Jimmy.

Roger: Hey, young man, what's with putting a fire in the hornet's nest first thing in the morning? (He walks in the kitchen.)

Jimmy: Dad, I thought I'd be nice and cook for ya'll before we leave.

Roger: Yeah, that's nice, but you know she cooks in her own house, so hurry up so we can get this day started on the right foot.

Five minutes later, we all sat down and ate and told the kids that they get to stay with Grandma till we get back.

MyRanda: I'd like to go with you, Mom.

Rona: Honey, you mind if she comes?

Jimmy: No, if that's what she wants. We need to unpack some stuff and then we need to get going.

About an hour later, we said our good-byes, got on the road, and headed for Louisiana. Around mid-morning and one hundred miles down the road, I saw a man hitchhiking. He was a well-dressed man. He was tall and wearing a T-shirt, Levi's jacket, jeans, and a silver belt buckle that read '95 Texas Rodeos. He was clean-cut, so I didn't get any bad vibes from looking at him. I pulled over, he ran up to the car, and opened the passenger side and got in the car.

Jimmy: Hi, what's your name?
Mister: My name is Red.
Jimmy: Where are you heading?
Red: I'm heading to Harahan, Louisiana.
Jimmy: If you don't mind me asking, why you are heading that way?
Red: No, I don't mind.
Jimmy: By the way, my name is Jimmy.
Red: Nice to meet you. What a nice car you have.
Jimmy: Actually, I'm heading to Jefferson County, just past Harahan, Louisiana.

We started talking about this and that.

Red: You got family up this way?
Jimmy: No, I'm taking this car back to the owner.
Red: I see.
Jimmy: So why are you walking to Harahan?
Red: Well, I was in a car, but it broke down and didn't have the money to fix it, so I was going to walk home, and when I get the money to fix it and drive it back.
Jimmy: What kind of work do you do?
Red: I work in a church making chili, and that's how the church makes its money. I got to say, it's the best damn chili this side of Texas. Hey, if you want, when we get there, I can give you a sample.
Jimmy: Naw, I don't like chili.
Red: Is that right!

We made small talk the rest of the way there, and just after dark, we made it to the Louisiana state line.

Red: Hey, you mind when we get to my town, can you drop me off at the church?

Jimmy: Yeah, I don't see a problem with that. We need to stop at the next rest stop so I can talk to my wife—that's her in that van behind us—so I can tell her to go on to Jefferson, and I'll meet up with her there at a motel.

About a few miles down the road, I see a rest stop. I pulled over, and I walk back to the van.

Rona: Is everything all right?

Jimmy: Yes, dear. He asked me to take him to the church in Harahan, and I told him yeah, don't see a problem with that.

Rona: Then why don't we all go together?

Jimmy: Because I want you to go on and get a motel, and that way when I come later, we all can get some good sleep and head out in the morning.

Rona: OK, are you sure? You'll be by yourself, you know.

Jimmy: Yeah, but look at me, I might be out of the force, but I still have a body that's in shape and can still handle myself. Don't worry, I'll be fine, it should only be an hour at the most.

Rona: Do you want your gun?

Jimmy: Naw, I don't think I need it. We are going to a church. The house of God don't need guns in there.

Rona: OK, honey, be careful. I love you.

Jimmy: I love you too. I won't be long.

Rona took off as I stood there. I needed to get back on the road, so I got back in the car.

Red: Is everything all right with the wife?

Jimmy: Yeah, she's going to head down to Jefferson.

We got back on the road, and after a while, we hit Harahan, and Red told me how to get to his church. As I pulled up to the front of the church, I saw a white van pull away from the side with the lights off.

Red: Come inside.
Jimmy: No, it's kind of late.
Red: I thought you might want a hot bowl of chili.
Jimmy: I told you already, I don't like chili.
Red: That's right, I forgot, then let me introduce you my pastor, the
    father of the church.
Jimmy: Naw, that's all right. I need to get on the road.
Red: It only takes a few minutes.

I started to get a bad filling in the pit of my stomach that something's
wrong, but I dismissed it.

Jimmy: Can you bring him out here to see me?
Red: It's dark out here, he can't walk the grounds.
Jimmy: OK, if it's just for a few. I need to get going, OK?
Red: Yeah, no problem, I hear you.

As we walk up to the side of the church, Red did a secret knock.
A slot opened on the door, and he said, "Mad chili." As the door
opened, he walked inside while I stayed at the door.

Red: Come on in, I'll go and get the father.
Jimmy: No, I'll stand here and wait.

Looking at the kitchen, it was huge, and four people were in their
cooking something on the stove, and two men were standing at the
back of the room at another door. Red walked over to the old man
and whispered something in his ear, and the old lady looked up at
me and had a half grin. The two guys walked over to the other two
people and walked them out of the kitchen, and the old man walked
over and introduced himself.

Father: I want to thank you, young man, for bringing my son home.
Jimmy: Yeah, it would have been a long walk, and I was heading this
    way anyway.
Father: Come in and have something to eat.
Jimmy: Naw, that's all right, I'm not hungry. Thank you, sir.

Then the old lady, who looked like she had one foot in the grave, looked up and started to walk toward me, holding onto the stove to walk.

Red: Carry, hold on.

He turned and went to her and helped her walk over.

Carry: Sir, don't disrespect the father in the church. You call him Father.
Jimmy: Yes, ma'am. Sorry, Father, didn't mean anything by that. By the way, what's your real name, Father?
Father: My name is Lou.

Lou had on a black robe and a red cloth with a pentagon on it.

Jimmy: What kind of church is this?

Just then, I felt a thud on the back of my head and everything went dark.

Meanwhile, back at the motel, Rona and MyRanda were getting worried because a lot of time had pass by and there was no sign of me.

MyRanda: Where's Dad? Maybe something is wrong, should we go look for him?
Rona: No, we will wait till morning (is worried herself). Besides, your dad can take care of himself.

As she was saying that, Jimmy was being dragged down a flight of stairs. Jimmy woke up in a dark room a few minutes later, and a pin light was off to his right. A voice ask if I was married.

Jimmy: No, I'm not, I'm here alone.
Voice: You lie. Red says he knows you talked to your wife, liar. Does she know where you are?

Jimmy: Yes, she does.

Voice: How's that? You don't even know where you are, and I thought you said you're not married.

Jimmy: OK, you got me. Yes, *yes*, I'm married, and no, she knows what town I'm in, that's all.

Voice: Yes, that's right, that's what Red told us too. Now I want you to tell me where your wife is at.

Jimmy: I don't know.

Voice: Liar! You told her to go somewhere to meet up with you, now where was that?

Jimmy: I don't remember. She left me at the rest stop.

Voice: Liar! Stop lying, we need you to tell us where she is.

Jimmy, to himself: Fat chance.

Voice: Red said a motel, what motel is she at?

Jimmy: No, I don't know where she went, she didn't tell me.

Voice: Looks like you have blood coming out of your head. Tell us what we want to know, and we'll fix you up. Does that sound like a deal? Now where's your wife?

Jimmy: I DON'T KNOW WHERE SHE WENT! I was supposed to meet her at some fast-food place, I don't remember.

Voice: Liar, liar, liar! The faster you tell us what we need to know, the faster you get help.

Jimmy: *Zzzz, zzzz, zzzz.*

Voice: Damn, he's out cold, now what do we do?

Red: We need to talk to those damn guys about hitting so hard. I think it knocked a few screws lose.

Voice: You two take him to the other room and tie him down and search him and see if you find anything. And make sure that no one helps him.

When I woke up, I could not move, so I yelled: Hey, let me up!

Girl: Shhh, they'll hear you. Shhh.

Jimmy: Hey, who are you? Where am I? Why am I tied up?

Girl: Shhh! They'll hear you and come in and punch you in the mouth for speaking without them asking you something.

Jimmy: Hey, come here and untie me, little girl. (The girl shakes her
    head no.)
Jimmy: You come here. I know you can hear me. You over there, help
    me. (Again the girl shakes head no.)
Girl: You are going to get everyone punished, so shut up, you fool.

Just then, a guy walks in and punches me in the mouth.

Guy: We have rules in here: you don't speak unless we say so, unless
    you like getting hit.

And then he walks over and grabs the little girl by the window by her
hair and slaps her for thinking of helping me.

Guy: And the next one of you that looks at him will not like what
    we do, got it?

At that moment, Lou walks in.

Lou: OK, people, we have a new addition to our workers, and we'll
    see if he works out. If not, I'm sure he'll taste good.

Jimmy: Hey, what the f——! When I get loose, I'm going to f——
    you up, just know that.
Lou, looks at the guard: Didn't you explain the rules to him?
Guy: Yes (walks over and pops me again).
Lou: By the way, no one look or feed or help him till tomorrow, and
    make sure he gets in these clothes and hand his old clothes to
    my men. Now we get an early start today, so get up and head
    out.

Just like in school, they all stand up, turn toward the door, and head
out, and like clockwork, right foot then the other. After the last
woman walks out of the room, the guy says: Take this day and get in
line because we won't waste time with you (walks out).

Meanwhile, Rona and MyRanda is sleeping, and around 5:00 AM, Rona gets up and looks out the window to see if Jimmy is parked outside.

MyRanda slowly wakes up and asks: Mom, is Dad back?
Rona: No, he's not.
MyRanda: What are we going to do, Mom?
Rona: We are going back and see if we can find him, and talk to the police.
MyRanda: Why don't we call them now?
Rona: Because he might be broken down, it could be nothing.
MyRanda: OK, Mom, I'll get the van ready, and we can leave as soon the sun comes up.
Rona: Yeah, that's sounds good.
MyRanda walks over and hugs her mom and says: I feel everything's all right, Mom, be strong.
Rona: Let's go get Dad and then knock the shit out of him for not calling us and making us worried.
MyRanda: Yeah, he better have a good reason for not calling. Hey, Mom, can we eat first and get some coffee?
Rona: Yeah, that's sounds good.

Around 7:00 AM, we got in the van and head to the highway, on our way to Harahan, while looking for Jimmy or the car he was driving in.

Rona: MyRanda, what time is it?
MyRanda: 8:45, Mom, are we about there? Right?
Rona: Yes, it is the next exit, and we'll look for him there, and if you see a cop, let me know, OK?

As we drove through the town going up and down the streets, MyRanda says: Hey, Mom, there's a cop. Let's stop him and see if Dad's in jail.

Rona: Yeah, I see him (drives down the street and pulls in front of the police car).

Rona: Sir, can you help me? My husband came here last night, and he had a hitchhiker he was helping to get home, can you see if for some reason he got put in jail?

Sheriff John: What's your husband's name?

Rona: His name is Jimmy Stone.

John: Where does he live?

Rona: We live in Wichita, Kansas.

John: His DOB.

Rona: August 5, 1972.

John: OK, I'll call it in, so give me a minute.

MyRanda: Mom, come here.

Rona: What?

MyRanda: So does he know?

Rona: Don't know, he's calling it in.

John: Ma'am, what's your name and the other person with you?

Rona: I'm Rona, and this is my kid, MyRanda.

John: Do you know the guy that was with Jimmy?

Rona: No, I saw him but didn't get his name, but I remember what he looked like. And I told you, he was a hitchhiker, sir.

John: OK, hold on a minute (and he puts his ear to mic).

Dispatch: There's no one here under that name or DOB.

John: 10-4. No, ma'am, there's no one in jail under that name, and I think you should go back to where you are staying and wait for him. He should show up soon. Really, I can't do a missing-person report till seventy-two hours has gone by.

Rona: OK, we will look for a bit longer and go back to the motel. Here's the room, number 07, and can you call me at ***-***-**** if you see him around?

John: Yes, ma'am, if I get a person with that name, I'll call you and hold him till you get here.

Rona: OK, then, thank you, sir, 'bye.

John: You're welcome, 'bye.

MyRanda: Mom, what are we going to do?

Rona: We will comb the town and see if we can find your daddy, and then go back to the motel.

About three and half hours later, they found the car sitting behind an old barn halfway in a ditch.

Rona: We should go get John and see if he can do something now.

They headed back to town. When they got there, she went to the police station. They went inside to the front desk.

Rona: Is Sheriff John in?
Front desk: No, he's out on patrol and doesn't come in unless he has to be. Is there something I can help you with?
Rona: Yeah. Officer Beth, isn't it? Can you have Officer John call me, he has my number. It's important.
Beth: Yes, ma'am, I'll do that now.

Five minutes later.

Beth: We can't reach him on the horn, I'll have him call you when he gets in.
MyRanda: OK, let's go, Mom.

Meanwhile, Jimmy looks up and see the sun going down. The other people starts to come in and line up at the wall. Two guys come in and walks down the line and tells everyone to sit down and not to move till they leave.

One lady: What about that man there? Father told us not to help him, but he said to get him out of those clothes, so do we help him or not?

The guy looks over and backhands this old lady.

Guy: Yes, you worthless piece of shit, you do what you are told.

The two of them walk out. A few minutes later, they all got up and came over and untied me and handed me the clothes to put on. The kids walk over to the corner, and the adult women turned their backs to me.

Old lady: Hurry up, they will be in a few to get the clothes.
Jimmy: What if I refuse?
Old lady: They will beat all of us, including the kids, so please put
    them on, mister.

So I start to take off my clothes and put the other ones on when one of the women drops down, crying softly. I hurried up and changed and put the clothes by the door.

Jimmy: There, I'm done. Stop crying, I'm not going to get you hurt,
    OK?.
Little girl: Shhh! I think I hear Tom and Frank coming.

Everyone walked to the wall and sat down as the door opened. They grabbed the clothes and walked out, looking at everyone as they closed the door slowly. Jimmy walked over to the women and asked if anyone could tell him what's going on here.

One little girl walks over and says: I'll tell you, but you have to be
    quiet.
Jimmy: OK, so why won't they talk to me?
Girl: Do you blame them? They have been beaten by those guys for
    weeks and some for years. I'll start with this—did they tell you
    if you are a worker or meat?
Jimmy: What are you talking about?
Girl: Do you know what the main ingredients for their chili?
Jimmy: No, I don't.
Girl: It is all of us.
Jimmy: *What!*
Girl: Shhhhh! I told you I'll tell you, but you need to keep it down.
Jimmy: OK, I'm trying.

Girl: As far as I know, eight years ago, Father's dad was the Father of this church. The current Father was in a cult then, and when his dad died, he took over. When he buried his dad, all his friends moved in. At that point in time, when people pass through this town and stayed the night, they would end up missing and end up here. Most of the time, the men would be killed right off the bat, and the kids and women would be put to work down here. The kids would have to put on a show of good girls to the public, and the teens would be sold to the strip club, or that's what I heard from Tom and Frank talking one day. So about five years ago, they started making chili, and we all would have to put up tables and sell it to the public to make money for the church. About two years ago, I was bought down here. My mom and dad were killed in front of me, and Father told me not to cry, my mom and dad will be in me soon, and when I asked what that meant, Father said, "Chili, of course, everyone that dies here gets chopped up and then put into the chili mix." We only get fed chili, and then when we go up the stairs, we package the chili for sale, and if we get out of line, we get beaten or killed.

Jimmy: Are you telling me, you were fed your parents?

Girl: Yes.

Jimmy: What a monster! He has to pay for his dues to the man upstairs.

Girl: If you are referring to God, there is no God because if there was a God, he would have stopped this madman.

Jimmy: Don't say that! God works in mysterious ways that no man can. Maybe that's why I'm here, just don't lose faith.

Girl: I'll try, but I lost faith a long time ago.

Jimmy: Yeah, that can happen, but all you have to do is open your heart to God.

Girl: I'll try.

Jimmy: That's the thing. God will wait till you are ready to let him in.

Girl: OK.

Jimmy: Has anyone ever escaped? And that no one suspects the church or the goings on here? What about the cops?

Girl: Yes, and one guy got out, but the sheriff shot him. I found out that the sheriff is Father's son, so this is a tight network. There's one way in and one way out—your death. It's late, and morning comes pretty early, so get some sleep, and remember, you don't look at them, you don't talk to them, and you don't make noise.

Jimmy: OK, thanks, little girl. By the way, what's your name?

Girl: It don't matter what my name is, you won't be here long enough to use it, or I won't be here to hear it.

Jimmy, trying to take this all in, but couldn't see how this could be happening.

Jimmy: It's morning, not that I got much sleep.

Tom and Frank comes in, waking everyone up: Get to the wall now!

And just like before, they all lined up and walked out with their heads down. As I walked to the door, I decided to look around the room.

Tom: Keep your head down and walk.

Jimmy: Why should I?

Frank: Why you ask! Well, why is this (punches me in the back and grabs my hair and pops me in the nose)! That's for talking, and this is for breaking the rules. Now get up and get in line.

The girl looks at me and gives me a quiet motion to come on.

Tom: Ain't it about time we sell another girl?

Jimmy: Leave her alone. You want to hit someone, hit me, but leave her alone.

Frank: Look here, we have a dipshit that does want to get hit and not follow the rules.

So right there, they started punching me, kicking me, and knocking me to the floor.

Tom: Now get up, get in line, so we can get to where you need to be.

Jimmy, thinking: If I plan on escaping, I need to find the layout of this place.

I got up and got in line and walked with the others. We all went up the stairs to the main floor and walked across the worship hall to the front of the church, to the right through a door, and back down the stairs to where a room had hooks of bodies hanging from the ceiling. There were tables that you chopped the bodies on and slid the parts into a pan and then take it to the kitchen.

Meanwhile, the sheriff finally comes into the station.

Officer Beth: John, a woman named Rona came in and said you need to call her, and it is important. She said you have her number.
John: OK, I will call her in a few.
He walks to his office and sits down and calls her.
Rona: Hello?
John: Yes, ma'am, this is Officer John. You needed me to call you, I have not seen anyone as of yet.
Rona: Yeah, that's not why I'm calling. We were driving around and found my husband's car out on Route 5 behind a barn.
John: What kind of car was it?
Rona: A green '72 Impala.
John: Did you get in the car?
Rona: No, I thought if I did, it would mess with evidence.
John: It's not a crime scene.
Rona: You don't know that yet!
John: Yes, ma'am, I do, unless you found a body. Did you?
Rona: No, there wasn't a body there that I saw, but it looked like someone searched through it.
John: OK, I'll head out there and find the car and look it over, then go from there.
Rona: OK, thank you, sir, will you let me know what you find?
John: No problem, it's all in a day's work.
Rona: OK then, I'll talk to you later, 'bye.
John: OK, I will. 'Bye, ma'am.

John gets up and goes to his car and heads to Route 5 to check out the lead. He arrives at the barn and runs the VIN number, and dispatch tells John the car was stolen and the owner is David, out of Jefferson County.

John: I'm going to the church.

John gets in his car and heads back to town. He pulls up to the church and walks to the back and knocks on the door. Red comes to the door.

Red: What you want?

John: I want to see my dad, is he busy?

Red: Yes, he is, I'll go get him.

Father comes out and gives his son a hug.

John: Hi, Dad, are things going well?

Father: Yeah, so why are you here?

John: Well, there's a lady that came to town, and she is looking for her husband, and she found his car, so I was wondering if by some chance you got someone new last night?

Father: Yes, we did, and what's her husband's name?

John: David.

Father: That's not us, so get rid of her. Do whatever you have to do to make her go away.

John: Hey, Red, if you're going to get rid of a car, at least hide it better than you did.

Red: Don't tell me how to ditch a car. It was dark.

John: Yeah, I'm sure the car had lights, and what's wrong with the rest stop where you put the cars before?

The sheriff leaves and goes through town and looks for Rona's husband.

It's been three days now, so the sheriff calls Rona.

John: Rona, if you are at the motel and if you are going to be there awhile, I was heading out to see you about some new information on your husband.

Rona: Yeah, I'm going to be here till I find my husband.

A few hours later, the sheriff shows up and knocks on the door to Rona's room.

John: Yes, ma'am, can you come out here so the kids don't hear what I have to tell you? Ma'am, I've search the whole town, and four days ago, a man came into town and got on a bus that was heading to California. So maybe David was upset with you and left you. We've seen it hundreds of times where a couple fights and the husband leaves or the wife comes up missing.
Rona: *What!* Wait a minute, my husband's name is Jimmy, not David. Are you sure you were looking for the right person?
John: Ma'am, I found the car and called the VIN in. The owner's name is David, and you said he was the owner, so that's why I thought his name was David. I don't know the name of the guy who got on the bus.
Rona: I know that wasn't my husband that got on the bus.
John: Ma'am, you can't really say it wasn't your husband that got on the bus.
Rona: Yes, I can because I'm holding all the money, and he only had enough for a tank of gas.
John: Ma'am, I'm going to fill out a report that your husband has left you until new evidence shows up that says otherwise.
At that moment, Rona started to break down and cry hysterically.
John: Are you going to be all right?
Rona: I'm going to take a few days and go home.
John: There's nothing more you can do. It's tough, and it happens. All you can do is move on from here (hands her his card). If there's anything I can do to help, I'll try. Sorry, ma'am.
Rona thanks the sheriff.
Rona: No, I'll be all right. I'm going home, and I'll call around to see where he went.
John: OK, ma'am, I hope you find him soon, 'bye.
Rona: OK, I appreciate that, 'bye.

The sheriff gets in his car and leaves. Rona goes back into the motel room and tells MyRanda what was just said.

MyRanda: Mom, what are we going to do?

Rona: Not sure, but I'm calling Mom to come and get you.

MyRanda: *No!* I want to stay here and help find Dad.

Rona: OK, honey, if you think you can take it. Now we need to remember that guy's name. I know your dad, he writes down everything, so we need to get to his car and see if he hid his notebook. Once a cop, always a cop.

MyRanda: Mom, let's do that in a little bit.

John calls his dad and tells him that he has taken care of the problem and that they are going home.

Father: That's what I like to hear, son, now we can get back to business.

John: I was wrong about the name. I told you his name was David, not Jimmy. I messed up, sorry. Was that important?

Father: *What!* You fool, we need her here so I can kill her in front of him. Go get her, and the girl child. We'll sell her to the bar as a stripper.

John: All right, I'll turn around and get them.

Father: Don't mess this up, son.

John: I'm on it, Dad.

Lou hangs up, and John turns around and goes back to the motel. When he gets there, Rona has already left.

John: Shit, no. Now Dad's going to be mad shit! I'll wait till I get back to town before I tell Dad. I f—— up again. (He heads out again.)

Rona and MyRanda shows up at the car and goes through the car and finds Dad's notebook.

Rona: Yes, all right! Here it is. Let's see his last entry.

MyRanda: His name is Red and he lives at the church. Mom, isn't that right across street from the police station?

Rona: Yes, it is that's weird.

Rona thinks of doing a stakeout on both of them or, more important, the church.

Rona: MyRanda, we are going to Grandma's house and borrowing her car so we don't get noticed.
MyRanda: Mom, you want me to stay here? Or go with you?
Rona: Yes, I wouldn't leave you here and take a chance of losing you too.

Rona was driving to town, and while going to the police station to leave a message for John, she saw a tow truck pass her with David's car.

Rona: Beth, can you leave John a message for me?
Beth: I sure can, or do you want me to call him?
Rona: No, that's OK, I don't want to bother him.
Beth: Sure go ahead, what's the message?
Rona: Tell John that Rona and MyRanda are leaving and going home now, thanks for all your help, and please return the car to David since you have the car now.

After two days, they made it to Grandma's and told her everything that happened, and that they needed her car and they wouldn't be back for a while.

Rona: Do you mind watching the kids?
Patty: Of course not, they can stay as long as they need too. Yes, take my car. Do you want Grandpa to go with you, he has guns.
Rona: No, Mom, I think I would get further with what I have planned.

The next morning, the girls left to go back to find Red.
When the sheriff got back to town, he went to his office.
John: Better get it over with and call my dad and let him know.

Ring, ring, ring! Red picks up and says: Hello?
John: Hello.
Red: What do you want?
John: Can you get my dad? This is his son, and it's important.
Red: Yeah, hold on.

A few minutes later, Father: Did you get them, or did you f—— up?

John: I was too late by the time I turned around and went back for
    them, so I came here, and they had left me a message that they
    were going home to wait for him to show up on his own. It
    doesn't say where though, so I guess we don't have to worry
    about them no more, right?
Father: You might be right, or they might be trouble later on.
John: OK, Dad, I'll keep a watch out for them.
Father: For what! You can't even catch a woman and a child and bring
    them to me.
John: I know I f—— up, that won't happen again.
Father: You better not, or I'll wash my hands with you and chop you
    up and put you in the pot.

As Father was speaking this, John: Dad, it won't happen again, I'm
sorry . . . Dad, are you there? Damn, he hung up.

In the meantime, the little girl at the church overheard Lou on the
phone talking to someone about Jimmy's wife and kid and how they
were trying to catch them, but they got away and went home.

Girl: Hey, Jimmy, this is what I heard through the vent when I was
    cleaning the floors.
Jimmy: What are you thinking? That was dangerous, you could have
    been caught. I need to get out of here someway or somehow. I
    need to get to my family and protect them, and shut this place
    down as well.
Girl: I told you that no one gets out alive. Many have tried, but all
    failed.

Jimmy: There's always a way of escaping, but you just got to wait for
a loophole and the right time. I just don't want it to be too late.

Now it's been two months, and Lou comes in the cellar and tells all
of us the fall chili cook-off is coming up, and we all needed to clean
up the front of the church. He tells everyone that he won't put up
with any nonsense:

Lou: So if you want to see the outside then be willing to work (turns
and walks out).
The little girl walks over and says: What's with the look?
Jimmy: What look? I'm thinking.
Little girl: Yeah, I know, that's what's getting me worried.
Jimmy: Remember I told you, all we need is time and a loophole,
then a way out.
Little girl: And I'm sure those men will be out there too.
Jimmy: Yeah, I'm counting on that. (He tells the girl his plan.)
Jimmy: Now let's get some sleep.
Little girl: Hey, Jimmy, are you going to forget about us?
Jimmy: No, I am going to shut this place down and get all of you
help, I promise.

The little girl now goes to sleep.

Meanwhile, Rona is sitting by a café eating a snack and sees a man
who she thinks is Red walking down the street. Rona asks MyRanda
to walk down the street and bump into that man with the big belt
buckle and ask him his name and to make sure to be cute. MyRanda
gets out of the car and walks toward the man, walking straight into
him, knocking her down.

Red: Oh, I'm sorry for knocking you down, are you all right?
MyRanda: Yes, I'm all right. Sorry for not watching where I was
walking, what's your name?
Red: You need to be more careful, and my name is Red.
MyRanda: It was nice to meet you, Red, 'bye.

Red: 'Bye, hope to see you around.

Red continues to the corner and goes into a strip club. MyRanda walks to the corner and waits for her mom. Rona sees MyRanda and drives up.

Rona: Was that Red?

MyRanda: Yes, it was and he went into the club there.

MyRanda got in the car, and the both of them went across the street and waited for Red to come out.

MyRanda: Mom, what are we going to do with him?

Rona: I'm not sure, but we need to get him to talk about what he did with your dad. Let's hope we have time to come up with something before he comes out.

About an hour later, they came up with a plan.

Later that night, Red came out of the club, and the girls decided to walk up to him and started to flirt with him, and see if he wanted to go to a motel and get laid by both girls. Red, without a second thought, jumped in the car, and they went to a motel on the outside of town. When they got there, the girls hanged on Red, flirted with him, and rubbed their bodies on him all the way to the room.

Rona put Red on the bed and asked if he was into kinky stuff. She tells him that they would blow his mind if he let them.

Red: Yes, by all means, go for it, but before we do, I want to see what I'm getting, so take off your clothes (getting excited because of what's happening, or so he thought).

MyRanda walks over to Rona and asks if they could talk in the bathroom.

Rona: Sure, honey. Red, just a minute, I have to talk to her first.

MyRanda: Mom, we're not going to have sex with him right?

Rona: No, honey, we need him to get relaxed with us so we can tie him up.

MyRanda: OK, Mom, I follow you.

Rona takes off her top and bra, and MyRanda follows what her mom did. Rona pulls out two sets of handcuffs, and MyRanda and Rona takes off his shirt, kissing his chest up to his neck, and then puts his hands to the post of the bed and cuffs him. Then they take off his pants and tie his legs to the bottom posts. That's when the girls went from sweet flirting girls to putting their clothes back on.

Red was thrashing around on the bed, trying to get lose and yelling: What the hell are you doing? Why are you putting your clothes back on?

Rona started asking about Jimmy. Red told them at first that he didn't know a Jimmy, and then the girls started smacking his lower body and chest with wire cords, he then told them that this guy Jimmy told him that he was going to leave them and go to California. (Red was starting to get a feeling that he was in deep shit.)

MyRanda: You are a liar, I know he didn't have the money to do that, and that he loves my mom and us kids.

For three days, Red stuck to that, and then he told them that when he left Jimmy, he went to the general store and that's the last time he saw him. On the fourth day, he broke down and told the girls what they wanted to know. (Not that it matters, the town and the law are in this together.)

Red, laughing: You two dumb bitches don't know the world of hurt you just opened. When I get loose, you there with the big boobs, you are going to die. And you there, MyRanda was it? I'm going to make you my prize bitch at the strip club.
Rona: That's the thing: we're not letting you loose. The room is paid for a week, and we're leaving you in here to die.

The girls took his clothes and went to the car and tried to think of a way they can save Jimmy.

MyRanda: Mom, what can we do?

Rona: I don't know. We need help, that's for sure, that's even if your dad is still alive. It's been months now.

MyRanda: Mom, don't say that, have faith in the Lord that Dad is OK, and we will get him back.

Rona: I'm going to the store and see if by some chance there was someone there that saw your dad.

MyRanda: Red said the whole town knows.

Rona: Yeah, I know, but I think Red would say anything to get rid of us, and we need to keep an eye out for your dad.

Meanwhile: Friday is tomorrow

Jimmy talks to the little girl about his plan and asks if she remembers what she has to do and how to make it look real.

Little girl: Yes: I got this. I'll put on a real show stopper and get every-one to come to me.

Just then, Father comes in with Sam and Eddy, and he tells everyone what they had to do and the time frame he wanted to have it done in.

Sam: Hey, you dip shit, you are raking leaves.

Eddy: And you dumb bitches are setting up tables and chairs.

Father: The little brats are going to bring out the chili.

The three of them walks out and shut the door and locks it.

The next morning, Sam and Frank comes in, kicking everyone: Get up and get to the wall.

Everyone went outside and was taken to where they had to work Four hours later, things were moving smoothly, and Jimmy looked a the little girl and nodded his head to do it.

The little girl comes out with a big pot of chili and slips on the grass. The pot flies up in the air and comes down on her leg. The girl starts crying out loud and screaming, "My leg!" All the guys and the Father goes to her, trying to see what happened. All the other women went over as well, to block Father and the guy's view so I could make my escape. I slowly walk to the back of the church and run to the first alley I see to hide till dark. I find a bunch of garbage bags and hid in them.

That's when Jimmy saw his wife sitting down at end of the block. Jimmy started running all kind of scenarios through his head and decided that it was too dangerous to let her know he escaped, in fear that she would get caught and be put in there as well or get killed. Jimmy ducked down and hid as tears ran down his cheeks, seeing his wife after all this time, and then fell asleep till dark.

Nighttime came, and Jimmy climbed out of the garbage and decided that he would go to the police station to see if he could get a policeman to listen to him about the church and the sheriff, since he never heard or saw the sheriff at the church. He thought that the little girl might be going on a scare from the guys that was holding them so they wouldn't escape. About then, Jimmy heard a noise from behind. As he turned around to see who it was, this old man stumbled down the alley, drunk to the tilt, making his way to Jimmy's spot. As he gets to Jimmy, he asked him if he knew where the police station was.

Drunk man: Yeah, it's over there next to the church. But if you are looking for the sheriff, then you need to go to the strip club, and you'll see him in there getting his nightly lap dance.
Jimmy: Damn! That means I have to walk past my wife or go the other way to the strip club and hope the little girl was wrong.

So I decided to go to the strip club to get the sheriff to help me. As I left the alley, being careful not to be seen by anyone, I went down to the club, not knowing who to trust. I walk in the club and look around to see if I could find the sheriff. I went to the bar.

Jimmy: Hey, have you seen the sheriff? I was told he was in here.

Bartender: Yeah, he's over there with that redhead at the corner booth (he pointed to him).

Jimmy: Thank you (walks over to the sheriff, sitting there getting a lap dance).

Jimmy grabs the sheriff's arm and yells: We need to talk.

Sheriff: What seems to be the problem?

Jimmy: There is trouble at the church. People are being enslaved and being killed and made into chili.

Sheriff tells Jimmy: Keep his voice down. Let's go outside, we can talk there.

John stands up, and the redhead falls to the ground. John and Jimmy walk outside. Jimmy tells John that for the past few months, he'd been held in the cellar at the church.

Sheriff: Sir, that's horrible, why you don't tell me the whole thing.

Jimmy: I was helping this guy get home, and he takes me to the church, and at that point, I was knocked out and dragged down to a cellar and was told I needed work for them or die. The man that is in charge is Lou, and they are taking people off the street and killing them or keeping them to work for him. And a few are sold to this place, and I was told that there was a cop that's helping them as well.

The sheriff looks at me like I was crazy and could not believe his ears.

Sheriff: Look, I've known the Father for years, and these accusations are farfetched.

Jimmy: Sheriff, look, if you don't believe me, I'll take you there and show you everything.

The sheriff calls the deputy on his handheld radio and tells them a code about the church. The deputy tells John that there is a call from the lagoon motel on Main Street that there's a man handcuffed to a bedpost. The caller says it's Red in the nude.

Sheriff: Leave him there for the night, I'm going to the church.

The deputy calls the church and tells him the code for "cleanup, the sheriff is on his way." Father cleans everything up and locks the cellar up and puts on his robe.

When the sheriff and Jimmy get to the church, they walk up to the doors and they hear singing coming out of the church, and they walk in and Lou is at the altar leading the choir. Jimmy looks puzzled.

Sheriff: Well, Jimmy, it looks like they are having church here.
Jimmy: Sheriff, let's go downstairs. That's where you will see everything that I was telling you about, and you will see that I was
telling you the truth.

The sheriff waves his hand for the Father to come over to them. Father asks if there's a problem or if there was there something he could do for them. John asks Lou for the keys to the basement.

Jimmy thought: That is weird, how does he knows that the basement
is locked?
Lou: I don't have the keys to the basement. If you want to cut the
locks off, you're more than welcome to do that.

As those two talked, I looked around for the little girl to see if she was in one of the pews, but she was nowhere in sight. The three of us walked through the church and then downstairs to the basement door to cut the locks off and look around.

John walks in there and says: It looks like it's empty to me.

That's when Lou pushes me into the room and John grabs me, sweeps my leg, and knocks me to the floor. Then he walks out and Lou walks in.

Lou: As far as the little girl and the other children, they are in the attic.

He turns around and he gives me a look that says this is my last day alive, and then he walks out and locks the door. Jimmy hears them laughing as they walk away.

John tells Lou: That was close. If he didn't come to me and went to someone else, we might be in trouble.
Lou: You did good, son, by bringing him back.
Jimmy: I'm doomed for sure.

Meanwhile, Rona wakes up from all the flashing lights at the church and decides to drive by and see what all the commotion is about from down the street in hopes that they might be bringing out a body or Jimmy. Rona decides to be on the safe side and wait until it dies down and then takes a look around.

She drove to where Jimmy's car was and waited for a few hours. Later that night, Rona came back to town and went to the church, and all the lights were off and a white van was parked on the side with no one in sight.

John was at the motel trying to get Red untied from the bed.

Father told Carry to get a new batch of chili ready; he's going to have the guys go and tenderize some meat in a few.

Carry, gets up and walks to the kitchen and says: Where's Red? That worthless piece of shit, he is never around when you need him.
Father walks to the room where Tom, Frank, Sam, Eddy, slept at and says: I want two of you to go down and soften up Jimmy, but don't kill him yet, and make sure you don't bruise the good meat on him. The rest of you, bring down all the other workers from the attic and put them in the basement, except the little girl that's friends with Jimmy. Just leave her up there for the night.

Meanwhile, Rona didn't see anything that gave her a clue, so she went back to the car and was trying to think of a way that they can get in the church and not be seen.

Rona, thinking: If we don't come up with something soon, Jimmy would be lost for good.

Sheriff has Red free, and John asks how he got in that predicament.

Red: There were two dumb bitches that just signed their death card when I find them.

John started laughing so hard that he started crying.

Red grabs John's arm and pulls his gun and says: Don't think for a minute I won't shoot you.

John then backhands Red.

John: You f—— (pops Red in the nuts and grabs his hair and slams him into the wall)! You little turd! How dare you threaten me! I only put up with you 'cause my dad needs you.
Red screams as he charges at John: I'll kill you! (Picks up the gun and pulls it in sight of John.)

By that time, John moves to the bed and pulls his night stick out and pops Red in the neck, and then hits Red's arm with the night stick to get him to drop the gun, and then drops Red with a blow to his head.

John: I should just leave you here, but dad wouldn't like that, so I'll take you back to the church and let you sleep it off.

Jimmy is now spitting out blood and is sore all over. The women and children have been brought back to the room, and I crawl over to them and ask where the little girl was.

Jimmy: She's not here?

None of them would talk to me in fear that they would be beaten for telling me, but they all were whispering.

Father came in the next day with Sam and Frank and tells everyone that they have the day off.

Father: You two take Jimmy to that room and soften him up a little more.

I am being dragged out by my ankles.

Father, while walking behind me, says: The little girl will be on the chopping block tomorrow.
Jimmy mumbles: So she's alive then.
Father: Yeah, she is, but not for long though.
Jimmy: Where is she?
Father: She'll be here soon (rubbing his belly).

After a while, Father came in and told the guys to help me up and take me to where the drain pipe is. He tells them that it got clogged up with all the leftovers and to not let Jimmy fall through the drain.

Father explains: We give you the acid and lye to eat through the skin and bones, and then knock the rest down past the wire into the chopper.
Sam said to me: Don't fall off the ladder or you'll go to pieces. Oh and by the way, there's no way of turning the choppers off either, so don't get any funny ideas, Jimmy!

Meanwhile:

MyRanda asks her mom: Are we ever going to find Dad? It's been two months now, and we haven't heard from Dad or seen him here.

Rona: I don't know, maybe Red was right after all and your dad left or he's dead. I'm going to call Grandma from the market and ask if she's seen your dad or heard from him, and ask about the kids to see how they are doing.

MyRanda: Yeah, maybe he went there by now or at least called there, because I know Dad loves us all and he wouldn't just leave us like that!

Rona left the church and drove to the market to call her mom.

Rona: *Ring, ring, ring*! Damn, answer the phone, Mom!

Patty: Hello, how can I help you?

Rona: Hi, Mom, how the kids doing? Are they being good?

Patty: Yeah, they're doing fine. They miss you, so when are you coming home?

Rona: Has Jimmy came there or called you there yet?

Patty: No, I've not heard anything from that piece of crap.

Rona: Mom, I need you to stop that (crying).

Patty, now getting concerned: Honey what's wrong?

Rona told her mom everything that she found out.

Patty: Well, did you see him anywhere?

Rona: No, Mom, I'm really scared and worried that something bad has happened to him (still crying).

Patty: Then it sounds like he left and you need to realize that, and he's probably got a new girlfriend and is with her now. You need to come home and get your kids and move on and get your life back together.

Rona: But, Mom, I can't do that yet, there's too much here that don't make sense about Jimmy disappearing the way he did.

Patty: Yeah, but didn't you say Red told you a lot of things, and maybe out of all the scenarios, one of them was the truth.

Rona: Yeah, but my gut feelings tells me that's there something wrong with Jimmy, and I can't shake it (crying more now).

Patty tells Rona: It's OK, you go with your feelings. The kids will be
    fine here.
Rona: I'll talk to you later, Mom, OK?
Patty: You take care of yourselves, and stay safe.
Rona: I love you, Mom.
Patty: Love you too, honey.
Rona: I'll call you in a couple of days, 'bye, Mom.
Patty: OK, make sure you do that, 'bye.

Meanwhile, Jimmy was forced up on his feet and was being shown
how to get to the room that had the drain.

Sam looked at me and said: Do a good job, and we will be back in
    an hour or so to check on you (smacks Jimmy on the back of
    the head).

A few minutes later, Jimmy heard a voice coming from a vent in the
ceiling; it sounded like the little girl's voice.

Jimmy: Are you all right? And do you know where you are?
Little girl: Yes, I do. Father put me in the attic with everyone else, and
    I was told I'd be up here for a few days, for helping you escape,
    and everyone else was led out in the middle of the night. Jimmy,
    why are you back here, were you caught?
Jimmy: No, I thought you might have been mistaken about the sher-
    iff, so I went there to get help, and he brought me back and
    threw me in here. By the way, do you know anything about the
    drain.
Little girl: I told you the cops are dirty, why would you do that? Why
    didn't you listen to me? I told you, you wasted your chance of
    escaping.
Jimmy: I know, I didn't think it through and I got stupid.
Little girl: Where are you?
Jimmy: I'm down in the room where the drain is, do you know any-
    thing about it?

Little girl: Yeah, remember a few weeks ago when I was nowhere to be found? I was in that room, and that's why I came in with all those cuts that day.

Jimmy: Yeah, now I remember. Do you know where it goes?

Little girl: No, I know it goes down to the choppers, and past that, you drop a few feet to a drain with running water. Other than that, I don't know.

Jimmy: OK, I'll make my way up to you and get you out, and then we can escape together.

Little girl: No, you won't make it up here! You go, I'll be fine. They don't know that we have talked, so you go.

Jimmy: Hey, can you tell me your name before I go?

Little girl: OK, I'll tell you it. It's Andrea. Now go! I hear them at the door.

Father opens the door and asks: Who are you talking to, child?

Andrea: I was playing with my friends. (Father looks around the room. It was empty.)

Father: Child, your friend that you helped was caught. I came up here to see what the noise was and to tell you we have a treat for you. You get to watch us rip the meat off his bones.

Andrea started crying. Father smiled as he turned and walked out the door and locked it.

Jimmy turned and walked into the back of the room and saw all the bodies hanging from the ceiling on hooks, being drained of their blood. Right before he got to the back room, he saw Red hanging from a hook as well.

Jimmy: You poor bastard, you got what you deserve. I'll pray for you.

I was wondering why he was on the hook in the first place. When I opened the door to the back room, it was the worse smell that I ever smelled coming from there; it hit me like a ton of bricks.

At that moment, I started puking. After that, I walked over to the drain and started looking for a power line that went to the choppers so I could turn them off. I found the line; it went to a closet. I followed it and looked inside and saw there was a fuse box on the back wall. Just then, Frank came in and asked me, "What are you doing in there?" He grabbed me by the arm and slung me back to the wall. As I hit the wall, I grabbed his shirt and swung my fist at him. He looked at me like, what was that?

Frank, with both hands, pushed me into the wall and started hitting me in the gut. That's when I grabbed his head and gave him a head butt that knocked him back a few feet. I used the wall to kick him in the chest as hard as I could. He stumbled back to the drain, and then with all my might, I ran and dove at his feet, knocking him into the opening of the drain, and watched him fall into the choppers. I waited a few minutes, then I got up and went back to the room to turned off the power to the choppers so I could get past them and escape. I went over to where the antifreeze was and poured it all over me so I would be slippery enough to get through the choppers.

I went to the ladder and went down to the choppers. As I slipped past the blades, my shirt got caught on one of the blades. As the shirt started to tear, one of the spikes tore into my chest, and I started to bleed. As I was hanging from one of the spikes, I looked up and saw Sam standing there looking for me. He looked down and saw me hanging there, trying to escape.

Sam then turns and says: You're going to love this, I'm turning them on.

He goes over to where the fuse box is and turns the power on. Nothing happens.

Sam: What! I don't hear them running.

He opens the fuse box and sees the breaker is off.

Sam: You're mincemeat!

At that moment, I let go and dropped down to the blood-filled water. I grabbed my chest where I was bleeding. I was trying to stop the bleeding. I looked around and saw lots of decomposing body parts. I was horrified and yelled while I fell back into a wall of smelly decomposing guts with maggots all over them. I sat there for a minute. I noticed a head floating toward me, bobbing in the water, getting closer to me.

I gathered my thoughts and started down the tunnel. After a few minutes, I noticed the tunnel was getting smaller, so I dove down in the bloody water, making my way farther down the tunnel, till I came to what felt like some metal bars that was corroded with pieces of decomposing human flesh that was blocking the flow of water. I stuck my hands through the metal bars and used my hands and legs to pry a hole through the corroded bars and wiggled my way through the hole. Now the current was moving faster, so I let the current pull me down the tunnel to the end, and I landed in a culvert that lead to the river. I laid there on my back, catching my breath.

Meanwhile, back at the church, Sam went to find Father and tell him that Jimmy escaped again, that he went through the choppers and now is in the pipe that goes to the river.

Father: Didn't you try to stop him?
Sam: Yes, but before I noticed him, he was already past the blades.
Father: Go call John and have him go to the river and pick him up, and to make sure he's dead when he gets him here. Never mind, I'll do it. You'll do it wrong, anyway.

Father calls John and tells him to go to the river and pick Jimmy up and to make sure that he's dead when he brings him back.

Father: I'm done with this guy, and I want him dead.

John told Father: I'll do that as soon as I can. (John thinks he saw Rona at the post office.) I have something to check out first.

Father: Be quick about it, we don't need him getting away.
John: OK, Dad, I will.

As he pulls up behind Rona and flips on the red-and-blue lights, Rona see it's John behind her.

Rona, thinking: If Red was right, then I need to go to the county line so I'm safe to see what he wants.

Rona starts her car and drives away. John follows and runs the plates. About the time she hits the county line, she pulls over and steps out. John walks over to Rona. A second squad car pulls up. John tells her to hold on and walks to the other cop and tells him that he doesn't need back up, that he knows her, so the other cop drives away. John walks back to Rona.

John: You need to go on home, there's no need for you to stick around.
Rona: I'm still looking for my husband.
John: Well, you need to give that up or you'll end up just like your husband.
Rona, yelling: What do you mean? You know what happened to Jimmy?
John: Yes, he should be in about a thousand pieces by now and being put in a huge pot of chili, and if you don't want the same to happen to you, then this is your last warning: leave and don't come back. By the way, I think I had some chili at lunch. Come to think of it, it was good!
MyRanda: Mom, let's go, let's get away before he changes his mind and comes after us.

Rona turns around and walks toward her car while saying to John: You knew where my husband was this whole time? You are a really cruel and demented bastard!

John stands there laughing while rubbing his belly as Rona drives away.

Rona tells MyRanda: We need to get to the Highway Patrol in Norco and let them know what's going on here.

A few hours later, the girls made it to the Highway Patrol station. Rona went into the station, crying for help. The officer at the front desk asks Rona to calm down and tell him what was going on and why she was so upset.

Rona tells him about the sheriff in Harahan, that she believes the sheriff is killing people and killed her husband, and that he threatened to do the same to her.

The officer told Rona to hold on while he called the captain up and told him that there was a lady up here making accusations about the sheriff in Harahan. The officer gets off the phone and tells Rona that the captain was on his way and would be up there in a few minutes.

The captain comes out and walks over to Rona and tells her to follow him to his office, where they can talk.

Rona sits down in a chair and tells the captain the whole story about everything that had happened to this point in the past few months.

The captain gets on the phone, calls dispatch, and tells them to go to Harahan, and to send an unmark car to investigate the sheriff in Harahan. The captain then tells Rona to go home; when they have an answer, they will contact her.

Rona tells the captain that she would get a motel room and let him know where they would be at while they wait for any news from him. The captain explains that it could take a few days to find out what's going on, if anything at all.

Captain: We could have an answer in a few days, or it could take months, are you willing to stay at the motel that long?
Rona: Yes, however long it takes to find out what really happened to my husband, I'm staying put.
Captain: Ma'am, I understand that you are upset and wanting answers, but there is a process before we have any answers.
Rona: Yes, sir, you will know where to find me when you have those answers.
Captain: Ma'am, I will walk you out, and so you go to the motel and I can get to work on this.

Meanwhile, the sheriff was heading to Sellers Lake to find Jimmy and kill him.

Jimmy was up on his feet and looking around to find a way to stop the bleeding. He made a mud pack and then climbs the embankment and crosses the road. When Jimmy got to the top, he looked around and he saw an outhouse sitting a few feet off the road. He ran to the back of the outhouse to hide. A few minutes later, Jimmy saw the sheriff drive over to where he just came up from.

The sheriff was poking around the embankment; that's when I decided to sneak off through the trees and get some distance between me and him. After a while, I made it through the trees to a road on the other side where there was a cornfield. I went across and hid and ate some corn. I thought traveling at night would be better, so I went to sleep until dark.

Jimmy awoke just after dark and started to walk down the road to head out of town, or so he hopes. A few hours later, he got stopped by a state trooper. He's get out of his car and draws his gun on Jimmy. (His clothes were still covered in blood.)

The trooper yells: Get on the ground and put your hands up.

I did what he said and lay on the ground. The trooper came over and asked me what my name was: What's with all the blood, did you just kill someone?

Jimmy: I am Jimmy, and I've been imprisoned at a church. The Father there is killing people, and the sheriff is helping him do it.

The state trooper put cuffs on me and stands me up and walks me over to the car.

State trooper: That sure sounds like a story, because the report I got is a mask murderer has escaped from jail in Harahan.

The trooper then told Jimmy that he had a friend at that police station and that he never heard anything like that. He puts Jimmy in the backseat and walks around and gets in and starts driving. The trooper then calls it in. He gets a report that a guy named Jimmy has escaped from Harahan jail, and he should be considered very dangerous.

Trooper looks at me: I got just the place for you in Vidor.
Jimmy told the trooper: The blood you see is mine, and I didn't escape from jail, I escaped from a church.
Trooper: That's not what the report says, and besides the sheriff and I are old friends from our younger years, and I know he wouldn't put a false report on the wire.
That's when Jimmy thought: I am screwed for sure.

The trooper pulls out his cell phone and makes a call to someone named Kane and said that he had a prisoner that escaped from jail in Harahan and they would be there by morning.

Jimmy thought: Out of the frying pan and into the fire.

Meanwhile, Kane was telling his men to get ready for a new worker that the trooper picked up and was bringing in the morning.

The troopers in Norco got a call from the undercover squad that got sent to Harahan. They found the sheriff and followed him to a church; he has been there for some time now.

The chief went to the captain and told him the report he just got from the undercover cop in Harahan. He tells the captain to call the undercover officers, have them go and check out the church, and to let him know what they find.

Meanwhile:

It's almost morning now, and we just reached Vidor. There's nothing but flat fields. The trooper takes me to the work camp and walks me in. I see two big buildings and five big buses. The windows are all painted black.

There was no one in sight but the guards of the camp. After hearing some talking going on, the trooper came out of the building and this medium-tall man walked out behind him with a shotgun resting on his shoulder, and a gold tee that ran all the way down to his belly. The two side arms and the rest of the guards had shotguns as well.

This guy that came out said: I'm Kane and I'm in charge here, and you can call me boss. Here are the rules: you will work in the fields, and if you try to escape, you will be shot on the spot. All prisoners will sleep in these buses, and you don't get to say anything to the guards with guns unless it's to say "Getting a drink, boss," or "Need a piss break, boss," and you don't move unless we tell you to.

Kane then waves his hand for the guards to grab me and says: Hold him good now. The two guards standing on both sides of me, grabs me, and twists my arms so I bend over. Kane then walks over to me, takes his gun, and puts it to my head and said, ejecting a shell: Is that clear?

Jimmy: Yes, it is.
Kane: What did you say? (Taking the butt of his gun and hitting me in the head.)
Jimmy, while seeing stars: Yes, sir, boss.
Kane, kneels down: Good, doggie (pats me on the head). Don't forget what I told you. Now take him to bus 1 so we can keep an eye on him.

The two guards drag me away.

The trooper walks over to Kane, and they walk over to one of the buildings that Kane came from. The guards got to the bus 1, unlocks the doors, and throws me in. They shut the doors and lock it. I hear the trooper talking to Kane but could not make out what was being said.

Meanwhile, Rona and MyRanda were at the motel crying because this whole ordeal was making them emotional over what they were going through.

The undercover officer called the chief and told him: While investigating the church, we came across a smell of something foul in the air. We went to see where it was coming from and went to the back of the church. That's when we saw the pastor and the sheriff cutting up little children and putting them in cooking pots. Do you want to take them down or wait for back up?

The chief told them to hold on for back up but keep an eye on them. The chief went and reported to the captain on the investigation.

Captain: Call the dispatch and have a squad go down to Harahan and take down the sheriff and anyone else that's involved with this criminal act.

The chief calls the undercover officers and tells them to wait till the reinforcement to come down there. The captain then goes to the motel where Rona was at and tells her what they found.

Captain: At this time, it looks like everyone that was at the church is presumed dead. You need to leave you information where we can contact you when we get done sorting out all the bodies. The DA will want to talk to you. You need to go home now and begin the healing and grieving for your loss. I'm sorry for your loss, but if you don't mind me saying this: go to God for your salvation and healing of the heart.

The captain goes back to the station.

Meanwhile, Jimmy hears the trooper get in his car and pull away.

A few minutes later, I heard the locks being unlocked then the doors swung open. A voice came over a loud speaker telling everyone to come out and stand on the side of the buses. As I walked out, I saw two guards at each bus with their guns in hand.

Kane, standing in the middle of camp, was informing every one of the new prisoner.

Kane: Today, we need to get this month's shipment ready, so let's work them hard today. Move out!

Meanwhile, Rona takes the paper from the cop and went inside and started to cry. After telling MyRanda what was said, she started to cry as well. Her dad was dead. As they both sat on the bed, crying, Rona decided to call her mom and tell her mom that she will be coming home now and will be there to pick up the kids in a few days and will be going home.

Patty: So did you find Jimmy?
Rona: Yes, Mom, but I will explain when I get there.

Rona starts crying again and tells her mom that it's not good news and that they were going to stay for a day and tie up any loose ends.

Patty: OK, take care of you (hangs up).
Rona was crying even more now. She didn't want her mom to hear
    her or worry about her.
MyRanda: Mom, what are we going to do now without Dad?
Rona: We are going to look toward God and let him heal us. For now,
    we are staying for a day, and then we will head to Grandma's,
    and we will be there by Sunday.

MyRanda takes the report from Rona and starts to fill it out. She starts tearing up again about her dad. Rona sees MyRanda being emotional and starts crying hysterically. She walks over and tells her it was going to be all right.

Rona: Let's lie down and try to get some sleep.

Meanwhile, it was midday where Jimmy was, and it was hot.

The guards took us all to the fields to work. While working, I looked around and saw that a lot of the prisoners had missing limbs. A lot of them had pegs for legs and wood-carved hands for hands. That evening, the guards brought us back to camp and put us in the buses, except the food runners for each bus (they're the ones that have been here the longest).

When I got in the bus, I noticed that there were no beds but tubs, twelve of them, and they had green fluid in them, so I asked Johnny: What's with the tubs, and where do we sleep?

Johnny told me about the tubs, and when it comes time to go to bed, we get in these tubs and put these patches on. If the patches comes off or we leave the tubs before morning, the guards come in and shoot a limb off before taking a fatal shot.

Jimmy asked Johnny if anyone ever tried to escape before from here.

Johnny: Yeah, look around at all the prisoners that are here that have missing limbs, those are the ones that tried time and time again to leave and got caught. The guards shoot off limbs and replace them with wood as the new arm or leg. And the ones that get shot up, you will find them or part of them on the other side of the cornfield.

Jimmy: What do you mean?

Johnny: I've seen it once, Kane chopped up some bodies and put them on ice, and when the van comes to take the shipment, the meat goes too.

Jimmy: Would you help me escape if I find a way that wouldn't get anyone shot or killed?

Johnny: Yeah, if you take me with you. Any place is better than here.

Jimmy: Can you talk to the other people and see if they have any ideas that we might be able to use? Is there a way to hot-wire the buses?

Johnny: No, none of the buses have engines or batteries.

Jimmy: So what do we use for lights?

Johnny: We don't. When it gets dark, that's when we get ready for bed.

Jimmy: That sucks. Hey, what about the cornfield?

Johnny: No, it won't work. There are booby traps that gets turn on every night.

About that time, the runners came in and brought the food. But before I got my food—that smell, I know that smell. I think it's chili. When I got up to the runner, he hands me a bowl of chili.

Jimmy: No flipping way. Here too? The one thing I can't stand to eat is chili.

Johnny: Hey, if you don't want yours then can I have it?

Jimmy: By all means, have at it. If you only knew what's in it, you might not be so eager to eat it.

Johnny: Wait, what's wrong with the chili?

So I told everyone where I was at, the church where the father would chop up people and cook them in the chili and sell it to the public. That's when a heavyset man gets up, walks up from the back of the bus, and says: Hey, I know where you are talking about. It is a place up in Harahan, right? I escaped from there about a year ago.

Johnny: Hey, Bubba, why you never told us about that place?

Bubba: I didn't think anyone would believe me because I had nothing to back it up. That's why for the longest time, I didn't eat the chili.

Jimmy: By the way, does anyone know where the chili comes from?

Johnny: Yeah, there's a truck that comes once a week that has some church name on the door.

Jimmy: Hey, Luke, you do the inventory, right?

Luke: Yeah, I give the order to the officer that comes once a week, and two days later, the truck shows up with the shipment, and then we load his truck with corn before he leaves.

A few minutes later, the guards comes in and tells us all to get in the tubs. Everyone gets in the tubs. The guard walks to the middle of the bus and says: You are in this one, get in there so we can show you how to hook yourself up.

Jimmy looks at the guard and says: I can't get in the tub. I have a bad back, and if you put those patches on me, I won't be able to walk in the morning.

Guard: Yeah, you keep telling yourself that. You don't get up and work, you will be shot on the spot. Now get in, or else. (He pulls down his gun, pumps it, and points it at me, and with his other hand, he points at the tub.) Now get in.

The other guard comes up from behind me and yells at me: NOW YOU WORTHLESS SHIT, GET IN THE TUB!

All the other prisoners tells me to get in the tub before it gets really ugly. About that time, Kane comes in when he hears all the yelling.

Kane: What seems to be the problem? Do we get to shoot someone tonight?

The guard standing in front of me turns and says: The new guy don't want to get in the tub because he has a bad back, so what you think boss?

Kane: Let me see if I got this right, what you are saying is you want me to shoot you in the head, right?

Jimmy: No, boss, I don't want you to have any reason to shoot me in the morning.

Kane: I will shoot you now if you're not in the tub by the time I pull out my baby (putting his hand on his side arm).

Jimmy, so not giving me any other choices, I got in the tub, and they put the patches on me and turn on the system. Kane, walks over to me and looks at me and tells me: Now I know your new here, but let me tell you this: I don't care where you're from or why you're here, but one thing is for sure, my guards or I will not waste any time with you, but if you remember anything, remember this: we will kill you and not give it a second thought.

He turns and walks away, telling his guards to be more vigilant.

Meanwhile, the highway officers had taken down the sheriff and his Father and all the guys that were at the church. Then they went through the church room by room and took all the people to the hospital, and they found a few children in the attic, chained to the floor. This one little girl started telling the officer about this guy that had escaped; his name was Jimmy.

Little girl: Did he make it to you? Is that why you are here? Is he here? Can I see him now?

The highway officer told the little girl that he didn't know what she was talking about, but he called it in just the same. The officer goes and calls the chief that there was a man that escaped a few days ago and his name was Jimmy and he might need medical attention.

The chief asked the officer if he has seen car 107, if it was there, and if so, to see if his radio was turned off.

Officer replied to the chief: No, I have not seen that car or trooper in a while.

Chief: He was supposed to be working in that area tonight.

The chief then goes to the captain and gives him the report and told the captain that car 107 was missing. The captain goes down to dispatch and has them turn on the GPS to find him and try getting him on the horn. The captain sits back in his chair and thinks about calling Rona and to tell her that's there a good chance that her husband was alive.

A few minutes later, dispatch calls the chief and reports that car 107 was on his way back from Vidor and that's why they couldn't get in contact with him; he's out of radio range.

Chief tells dispatch: When car 107 gets back in range, have him return to the station and report to me.

Meanwhile, back at the motel, Rona wakes up and gets MyRanda up from their sleep of sorrow and fills out the forms from the trooper, crying the whole time. Rona was telling MyRanda that she didn't know how she was going to tell her brothers and sisters what happened to their dad.

MyRanda: With the grace of God, we need to tell them the truth and get the pain and death of our Dad out in the open and deal with it, instead of lying to them and having them resent Dad for leaving, or lying to them about Dad leaving.

Rona: MyRanda, that was very grownup. We need to pack up and head to the station to return this paper, so let's make the best of it and get the car packed, OK, honey?

MyRanda: Mom, can we get something to eat first? I'm starving.

Rona: That sounds good to me too.

They finally got everything packed and was heading to the highway patrol station to turn in the paper work. About halfway to the station, they got pulled over by a trooper, and he came up to the car and told Rona that she needed to follow him back to the station.

The officer escorted Rona to the station they went in to see what was going on. As they walked through the door, the captain was waiting up front and walked up to Rona.

Captain: We need to talk, come to my office.

After they made it back to his office, he asks them to sit. The captain starts to explain to them about the arrest of the sheriff in Harahan when the chief walks in, interrupts them, tells the captain that car 107 has just arrived at the station.

Captain, jumping up: We need to deal with this.

He excused himself from the room. The chief told Rona and MyRanda not to leave his office.

Rona: Is there something going on?

Chief: No, it's just an office matter. The captain will be right back, just sit there, and it won't be long.

Captain told Max (the trooper that drove car 107): We need to talk.

He took him to an interrogation room and asked him to explain himself, why he wasn't where he was assigned to patrol. Max told the captain that he had caught an escapee from Harahan jail and took him up to that work camp in Vidor and dropped him off.

Captain: What was his name?

Max: I'm not sure of his name.

Captain: His name, what was it?

Max: It was Jimmy, I think, not too sure.

Captain: Did you call it in before you left your post?

Max: Yes, sir, I called the Harahan sheriff and got back a report that said he was picked up for murder and he escaped from the jail.

Captain, with a puzzle look on his face: What work camp in Vidor?

Max, with a scared look in his eyes: The one that opened five years ago, sir.

Captain: Stay in the room, the chief will be in here in a few minutes to talk to you some more.

Max asks the captain: What's going on here?

Captain told Max: The sheriff in Harahan is being picked up for questioning.

Max: Who? John? He is an old friend of mine.

Captain: Is he now? That's good to know.

The captain left the room to go find the chief and told him to not let Max out of his sight or to let him make any calls. The captain went back to his office to finish talking to Rona.

Captain: Now let's get back to what I was telling you. The sheriff has been arrested and all the others that were involved. It appears there was a huge ring of people that was involved in the disappearance of your husband and others.

Captain looks at Rona (should I tell her about her husband that might be alive?): Is there any questions.

Rona, in a soft voice: Did you find Jimmy? Is he still alive?

Captain: It's still too soon to say. We have a lot to sort through before we have any answers, but you can go home now, and the DA will get in touch with you once we have all the evidence and let you know the details at that time. I wanted to assure you that you have nothing to worry about from the sheriff.

MyRanda stands up and says: So you're not going to tell us if my dad is alive? What's wrong with you! You can see that this whole ordeal has been a lot on us, and you sit there with the power to rest our hearts, and you're not going to tell us.

Captain: Ma'am, sit down. I'm sorry, but not at this time. We still have a lot of evidence to go through, and I don't think that it's a good idea right now.

The captain stands up and tells Rona and MyRanda: Look, something has come up, and I need to deal with it.

Rona grabs MyRanda. They left his office and went to their car as she cried. MyRanda starts to drive back to Grandma's house.

Meanwhile, the next morning, the guards came and turned off the sensors, and everyone got up except Jimmy.

Johnny: Hey, you need to get up.

Jimmy: Yeah, Johnny, I know, but I can't move. I told you my back was messed up.

Johnny: We only have twenty minutes before the guards come in and take us out to the fields.

Jimmy: I'm trying, but my legs won't move. I need help.

Johnny: Hey, Bubba, come here and help me get him up. Luke, you and the other guys run interference till we get Jimmy up and moving around.

Luke: What's in it for me?

Jimmy: You can have my chili tonight.

Luke walks up to one of the other guys and tells him: Let's make it a good one, huh?

The two of them start to push each other till they make it to the front of the bus, pushing and hitting each other hard enough to make it look real. Two guards came to the front of the bus to break it up. One

of the guards puts down his gun to grab the two that was fighting; one of the other prisoners grabs the gun and hides it. By the time they broke up the fight, Jimmy was up and walking to the front of the bus, telling Johnny: Thanks for not leaving me in there.
Bubba: We all have to stick together in this shit hole.

Kane comes out of his hut and tells the guards to get everyone out of the buses.

The guard that put his gun down yells: MY GUN, WHERE IS IT?
Kane: You better find it. Now, who started this fight? And whoever took the gun, give it up.
One guard: The fight was between these two piss ants (pushing them to the ground).
Because of the bond the prisoners had, they all said: We all did it, boss.
Kane walks over to Luke and says: We need a new food runner.

He then shoots him in the head and the guy next to him as well. Kane walks down to Jimmy.

Kane: This is your doing, isn't it?
Jimmy: No, boss.
Kane: I thought you said if you were put in that tub, you couldn't walk in the morning.
Jimmy: Yes, I did boss.
Kane: I was getting excited to shoot you, instead I had to shoot those two piss ants over there. TAKE THEM ALL TO THE FIELDS!

Then Kane called the two guards over to his hut, the ones that broke up the fight, and told them they had better find that gun before day's ends. The two guards went in the bus and went through it, but didn't find any gun (knowing that Kane will be mad if they come up with nothing).

The guards went to Kane's hut and told him that they couldn't find the gun.

One of the guards said: Maybe you shouldn't have shot Luke till we
    found the gun!
Kane: What did you say to me?
One of the guards said: Look, I know we have to keep these piss ants
    in line, I get that, but you fly off too fast, and now they have a
    gun, that's all I'm saying.
Kane: Look, I'm going to shoot as many as I want. They're all food
    anyway. You two's job is to keep me from shooting them by
    keeping order, so with that, find that gun.
Guards: Yes, yes, Kane.

Jimmy was out in the fields. It was getting hot, and since Kane shot
Luke, we don't have any water out here. (Damn, why did he have to
shoot them?)

Jimmy decided to ask: Can I get a drink, boss?
Guard: No, you can't. This is my water. Get to work.
Jimmy, whispers to Johnny: Damn, we need a few of those shells on
    his belt.
Johnny: Good luck on that, you can't even get close to them without
    getting hurt.
Jimmy: I have an idea. Boss, can I take I piss?
Guard: Yeah, get up and come here.

I get up and walk over to him. We walked over to the tree lines, and
when I was done, I turned and tripped and fell in front of him.

Guard: GET UP NOW!

As I got up, I grabbed the guard by the leg and pulled myself up. The
guard looks at me, and without a bat of an eye, he hits me with the
butt of the gun in the chest and said: Don't you ever touch me again.

Jimmy coughed: Yes, boss.

We walked back to the line and started working again.

Bubba looked at me and whispered: What are you doing, are you
    trying to get yourself killed?
Jimmy: No! Look, I got two shells from his belt for that gun.
Johnny: Yeah, what makes you think they didn't find that gun yet?
Jimmy: I can hope they didn't.

By nightfall, word had gotten around that we were making a break
for it; and there were ten shells for the gun now and a few shanks.
Bubba told me that Johnny told him that the other guys (when we
make a break for it) will all make a diversion, as long as we bring back
help and get us all the hell out of this shit hole.

Jimmy: Hey, send the word around that in two days, we'll make a
    break for it at night.
Johnny: How do we get out of these buses?
Jimmy: Look, when the guards come in to put the patches on. You,
    Johnny, are the closest to the front of the bus, we'll put the gun
    up by you, under your right side of the tub. As the guards walk
    down the bus, you hop out and sneak up behind them and
    stick the gun to his head. Bubba, you think you can snap their
    necks? So we can put them in the tubs and hook up the patches
    to them.
Bubba: Yeah, that's a great plan. I'm in.
Johnny: Yeah, me too, I'm in also.
Jimmy: OK, in two days, it's a go.

Two days have passed and everyone knows the plan. Tonight, it's do
or die.

The guards came in, and it went down without a hitch. As we were
making our way out of the bus, we heard Kane and all his men having a good time in the hut.

Jimmy: Ain't that good luck!

As we made our way to the other buses, breaking the locks off the doors, Johnny told them to keep it down till we got to the field. Jimmy and Johnny left through the tree lines, heading toward the highway. That's when Kane came out of his hut and saw all the prisoners coming out of the buses.

Kane told one of the guards to flip on the lights and turn on the alarm for the field. The guards all came out and rounded all the prisoners up with little to no fight, and stuck them all back in the buses. But when they got to the first bus, they noticed there were two guards that looked like they were knocked out, until they checked them for a pulse; they had none, and realized they were dead.

The guards came out yelling: There are dead men in there, and we are missing two piss ants, Kane.
Kane: Which piss ants are missing?
The guards said: Johnny and Jimmy are gone, and they killed two of the guards.
Kane: Spread out and find those piss ants, and make sure you bring them back alive. I got something very special for those two.

So far, Johnny and I have made it halfway down the tree line and went through it. We should be safe to cross the cornfield at this point. We got five feet into the field, and we kept hearing a whispering sound. Johnny told me to duck and pushed me down, and at that moment, a wire whips by and off went Johnny's head, rolling on the ground and landing right next to my face, staring at me. I sat there, doing a silent prayer for my friend for giving his life up to save me.

Kane snuck up behind me quietly and said: If you value your life, you will stand up and not move.

At that moment, I felt a sharp pain in the back of my head, and everything went black. After they got me back to camp, I got woken up with ice water into the face. I tried to move, but couldn't; I was tied down to a table in Kane's hut.

Kane comes in, walks over to me, and says: Great, you're awake. I wanted you to see what I'm going to do to you. Let's see, what to do to you? I know, since you like to run, let's put a stop to that.

He picks up a chainsaw and cuts off my right leg at the knee and screws in a wood peg. He blow-torches the rest of the cut and had the guards drag me to the bus.

The next morning, Kane had all of us come out to the court yard to give us a speech on what happens when you get an itch for escaping and what it does to you. Kane then called me out to the middle to show everybody what he did to me and Johnny. He pulled Johnny's head out of a bag and held it high so everyone can see it.

Kane told me to get back to the bus. As I limped by one of the guards, I grabbed his gun and shot Kane in the chest.

Kane, while laughing: You can't hurt me, I wear a bullet proof vest under my coat at all times.

At that moment, everything went black. I woke up a few hours later on the floor of the bus. Jimmy: Man, my head hurts, and my hand feels funny.

As I got up, I notice my right hand was killing me. I look down, and I had a wooden-carved hand. I was in the bus all day by myself.

Meanwhile, the captain called a meeting for the troopers.

Captain: We have Intel on an illegal prison camp over in Vidor. I need about a dozen of you to go over there and bust them with the SWAT team.

Meanwhile, Jimmy is waiting for everyone to return. It was getting dark. At that moment, the doors open and the prisoners come in. As soon the doors shut, the state highway troopers shows up.

Jimmy heard a loud voice saying: Put down your guns, the place is surrounded!

Lights of red and blue filled the sky, and the guards started shooting at the troopers until the SWAT team started taking them out and then put the rest of them into custody. Kane saw what was happening and left. Jimmy saw Kane run past his hut and into the tree lines.

Troopers open the buses and got all the prisoners out of them, and while standing around outside, I decided to duck and disappear once again into the tree lines.

I made my way across the cornfield (no alarms were on) and through the riverbed to the Texas state line and headed to my mother-in-law's house. Little did I know Kane was following me.

A few days went by, I finally made it to Mom's house. I open the door, and Mom looks right at me.

Patty: What the hell happened to you? I thought you left Rona and the kids high and dry for another woman.

I started telling her everything that has happen to me. At that moment, a news bulletin came across the TV announcing about the church and the ties to the fake prison camp being taken down and all involved arrested, but it appears that one had escaped and was on the run. Authorities believe his name was Kane. Mom asked me if I was involved in that mess too.

Jimmy: Yeah, Mom, I barely got away with my life.

That's when we heard a knock at the door. I thought it was Rona. Roger got up and answered the door. As he opened it, a barrel came straight in his face. It was Kane, standing there with his gun.

Kane, yelling: You have something of mine, send him out now!
Roger: Who do you want? I don't have anything of yours.

He grabs a pistol off the couch and hands it back to me, and I put it on my back side under my shirt.

Kane: Send out that piss ant with the wooden leg now, I won't ask again.
Roger: Hold on, let me get him.

Roger turns, looks at Pat, reaches under the couch cushion, grabs a gun, and holds it to his back (Mom, call the cops.)

Kane walks in, pointing his gun at all of us and then pulls out his pistol and shoots the phone.

Kane: Let's not get stupid, all I want is him (pointing his gun at Jimmy).

As I walk past Roger, he whispers: As soon as you get a shot, take it.

Kane and I were walking down the driveway.

Roger came out and yelled at Kane: Hold on, son, the cops are on their way.

At that moment, Kane turned around and looked at Roger. He pulled his shotgun to shoot him, and I pulled out my gun and shot Kane in the knee, the back, and left shoulder.

Kane went down.

Jimmy took off running (if you call it running) into Mom's house. At that moment, Rona and MyRanda showed up and got out of their car. They didn't see Kane lying there in the dark. As they walked up to the door, Kane reached out and grabbed MyRanda and held a gun to her back.

Kane: I got this child, I'll shoot her if you don't come out now!

Roger, still in the dark, sneaks up behind Kane, knocks the gun out of his hand, and punches him in the left shoulder. As Kane reaches for his shoulder, Roger grabs MyRanda and pulls her away. Rona picks up the gun and shoots Kane in the head.

Rona: DON'T YOU EVER TOUCH MY KIDS AGAIN, YOU BASTARD!

Just then, Jimmy came out! Rona saw him standing there and started crying in disbelief. Was this Jimmy? As she walked over, she realized it really was Jimmy. She cold cocks him one right in the face while yelling: DON'T YOU EVER DO THAT TO ME AGAIN, OR I'LL KILL YOU MYSELF, ASSHOLE!

That's when the cops showed up.

Cop: What's going on here?
Jimmy: We did your job for you, and ya'll a dollar short and a day late. Take him away.

The next thing I knew, I woke up in my bed in a cold sweat and checking all my limbs and looked for any cuts. There were none. As I walk out of my room, I realize it was a dream. I went to my wife and kids and told them of the dream I just had and how real it felt.

THE END

ABOUT THE AUTHOR

The author, James Goodenough, has had many trials in life. He has a family and has been blessed in good times and has had bad times in life. He lost his daughter at a young age. He has told his kids, "The world is your oyster, and if you work hard at it then it can happen for you," and this book is proof of that. When James wrote it, he was going through a rough time. He had broken his back in four places and could not do much of anything, so one day, with the help of his wife, he wrote a book. For years, he's tried to get his book out there. As time passed, he thought that this day would never come.

James Goodenough was born in the later '60. He has lived in many places and has done all kinds of work. He is one of nine kids and has taught his kids that nothing is more important than family. Friends 'll come and go; jobs will come and go, but family will always be ᵉ for you.